The Old Woma
and Her Pig

A Traditional Story retold by Mary O'Toole

Illustrated by Chris Meadows

M

An old woman went to market
and bought a pig.
Pig had four legs,
but pig would not go.

'Well,' said the old woman. 'What shall I do?'

She went a little further
and she called to a dog,
'Dog, dog, bite pig!
Pig won't go,
and I should have been
at home two hours ago.'

But the dog would not bite pig.

She went a little further
and she called to a stick,
'Stick, stick, beat dog!
Dog won't bite pig,
pig won't go,
and I should have been
at home two hours ago.'

But the stick would not beat dog.

She went a little further
and she called to a fire,
'Fire, Fire, burn stick!
Stick won't beat dog,
dog won't bite pig,
pig won't go,
and I should have been
at home two hours ago.'

But the fire would not burn stick.

She went a little further and she called to some water,
'Water, water, quench fire!
Fire won't burn stick,
stick won't beat dog,
dog won't bite pig,
pig won't go,
and I should have been
at home two hours ago.'

But the water would not quench fire.

She went a little further and she called to an ox,
'Ox, ox, drink water!
Water won't quench fire,
fire won't burn stick,
stick won't beat dog,
dog won't bite pig,
pig won't go,
and I should have been
at home two hours ago.'

But the ox would not drink water.

She went a little further and she called to a butcher,
'Butcher, butcher, kill ox!
Ox won't drink water,
water won't quench fire,
fire won't burn stick,
stick won't beat dog,
dog won't bite pig,
pig won't go,
and I should have been
at home two hours ago.'

But the butcher would not kill ox.

She went a little further and she called to a rope,
'Rope, rope, hang butcher!
Butcher won't kill ox,
ox won't drink water,
water won't quench fire,
fire won't burn stick,
stick won't beat dog,
dog won't bite pig,
pig won't go,
and I should have been
at home two hours ago.'

But the rope would not hang butcher.

She went a little further and she called to a rat,
'Rat, rat, gnaw rope!
Rope won't hang butcher,
butcher won't kill ox,
ox won't drink water,
water won't quench fire,
fire won't burn stick,
stick won't beat dog,
dog won't bite pig,
pig won't go,
and I should have been
at home two hours ago.'

But the rat would not gnaw rope.

She went a little further and she called to a cat,
'Cat, cat, kill rat!
Rat won't gnaw rope,
rope won't hang butcher,
butcher won't kill ox,
ox won't drink water,
water won't quench fire,
fire won't burn stick,
stick won't beat dog,
dog won't bite pig,
pig won't go,

and I should have been
at home two hours ago.'

Then the cat began to kill the rat,
the rat began to gnaw the rope,
the rope began to hang the butcher,
the butcher began to kill the ox,
the ox began to drink the water,

the water began to quench the fire,
the fire began to burn the stick,
the stick began to beat the dog,
the dog began to bite the pig,
and the pig began to go.

And so it was all over.
The old woman
who went to market and bought a pig
got it home at last.